D1052161

THE MYSTERY IN Hawaii

Managing Editor: Sherry Moss
Assistant Editor: Gregg Adams
Cover Design: Vicki DeJoy
Content Design: Randolyn Friedlander

*We have elected to forego using the glottal stop ('okina) in the text of this book. It benefits most
young readers to not add the extra character to the Hawaiian words. Children will learn the
intended meaning of the Hawaiian words through context usage.*

Gallopade International is introducing SAT words that kids need to know in
each new book that we publish. The SAT words are bold in the story. Look
for this special logo beside each word in the glossary. Happy Learning!

Gallopade is proud to be a member and supporter of these educational organizations
and associations:

American Booksellers Association
American Library Association
International Reading Association
National Association for Gifted Children
The National School Supply and Equipment Association
The National Council for the Social Studies
Museum Store Association
Association of Partners for Public Lands
Association of Booksellers for Children
Association for the Study of African American Life and History
National Alliance of Black School Educators

Once upon a time...

Hmm, kids keep asking me to write a mystery book. What shall I do?

Mimi

Write one about spiders!

Papa said …

Why don't you set the stories in real locations?

That's a great idea! And if I do that, I might as well choose real kids as characters in the stories! But which kids would I pick?

MiMi, PiCK ME, PiCK ME!

ME, TOO, MiMi, PiCK ME, TOO!

Christina

Grant

Pick me!

You two really are characters, that's all I've got to say!

Yes you are! And, of course I choose you! But what should I write about?

National Parks!

Scary Places!

Famous Places!

FUN PLACES!

Disney World!

New York City!

Dracula's Castle

GRAND CANYON

On the *Mystery Girl* airplane ...

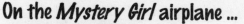
I CAN FLY US anyWHERE!

Or aboard
the *Mimi!*

Take me to the
Forbidden City!

Or by surfboard,
rickshaw,
motorbike,
camel ...

All great ideas!
I can put a lot of history,
MYSTERY,
legend, lore, and laughs in
the books! We can use other boys and girls
in the books. It will be educational and fun!

Good
stuff!

And can you put some cool stuff online? Like a Book Club and a Scavenger Hunt and a Map so we can track our adventures?

Of course!

And can cousins Avery and Ella and Evan and some of our friends be in the books?

Of course!

9

And so, Mimi, Papa, Christina, and Grant took off aboard the *Mystery Girl* and America's National Mystery Book Series—where the adventure is real and so are the characters! —was born.

START YOUR ADVENTURE TODAY!

READ THE BOOK!

GO ONLINE!

Yikes! That was close!

TRACK YOUR ADVENTURES!

APPLY TO BE A CHARACTER!

Rats!

Heading for Hawaii
by Grant

     We are going to the Hawaiian Islands. It sounds exciting. Of all the states, Hawaii must be the most exotic (Mimi would say) and the most "geogologically dramatic" Papa said. Christina and I just think it sounds like paradise. I guess folks just sit around on the beach all day? I know Mimi will make us learn Hawaii's amazing history. And I know Papa will tell us all about that "Day that will live in Infamy." I don't know where Infamy is, but I guess if we go to all of the islands, I will find it.

Honolulu International Airport, Honolulu, HI

Christina looked out the window of her grandparents' plane, the *Mystery Girl*, and marveled at the landscape below. It seemed so exotic and strange, in an exciting way. She couldn't wait to reach land and experience the sights, sounds, and smells of Hawaii!

It seemed like a year ago that they began this trek across the globe. Even though she and her brother Grant loved traveling on the *Mystery Girl* with Mimi and Papa, the plane seemed to grow smaller and more cramped by the hour during this long flight.

Having flown to California before, Christina knew that it was 2,000 miles away from home. She had no idea that it was another 2,500 miles from California to Hawaii! "Are we there yet?" had taken on an urgent meaning to her.

Grant and Mimi had been asleep for a while and Papa was intensely focused on flying. Christina patiently watched for the ocean to turn from blue to "the most amazing shade of turquoise you've ever seen," as Mimi had described it.

Normally, when Christina and Grant traveled with their grandparents it was because Mimi was working on a new kids' mystery book. She had decided that this trip would be mostly vacation, with just a "little bit" of writing on the side. ("Ha! Ha!" Papa had said, not believing that in the least.)

They would fly into Honolulu first and stop over for two days of sightseeing. Then it would be off to Maui, where they could relax on the beach before flying to see the other islands. Relaxing on the beach sounded like a waste of time to Christina, especially after how long it took to get there.

To keep her mind off the length of the flight, Christina tried to visualize palm trees being gently blown side to side by the trade winds.

She thought about how fun a real luau must be! She wondered how exhausting it would be to hike to the top of Diamond Head, the most famous volcanic crater in the world.

Her smile faded to a look of concern as she fretted about Grant possibly falling into the crater! Falling into stuff is something her little brother excelled at!

She also wondered if poi, the mushy paste food that Papa had warned them about, was all that Hawaiians ate. How would she survive that?!

All of a sudden, she was jolted back into reality by the growling sound of the plane's engines slowing down. Christina looked out the window and saw the incredible turquoise water Mimi had told her about.

"Aloha!" Papa announced loudly, "welcome to Hawaii!" as they descended toward a landing at Honolulu International Airport.

It's about time, Christina thought.

"I don't know about anyone else," Papa shouted over the engine roar, "but I'm starving. Let's go get us some poi!"

"I'm starving too, Papa," said Grant, stretching and rubbing his tummy. "But what's poi? It's not like poi-SON, right?"

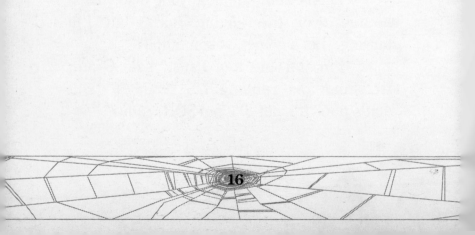

1
HOTEL HULA

Grant rubbed his blue eyes in wonder as they approached the entrance to the Royal Hawaiian Hotel, the oldest hotel on the Island of Oahu. His blond hair was more tousled than usual because of the long trip. He had stayed in many hotels with Mimi and Papa before, but this was different.

"Look, Christina," said Grant. "It looks like a big, creepy bottle of Pepto Bismol!"

"Maybe that's why they call it the Pink Palace," Christina replied. Tall and lean, with medium length dark hair and blue eyes, Christina towered over her younger brother.

Mimi and Papa were looking forward to staying in a hotel with such a rich history, but

Christina and Grant thought any hotel built in 1927 was just OLD!

Papa, looking handsome as always in his cowboy hat and boots, sauntered up to the registration desk.

"Name on the reservation, sir?" the desk clerk inquired.

"Papa, cowboy pilot of the *Mystery Girl*!" he replied proudly.

"Uh, actually, the reservation is under Carole Marsh," Mimi said. She wore a brand new red suit with matching shoes that she bought just for this special vacation.

"Whatever the beautiful blond lady says," Papa said. "I just want to get this vacation started. By the way, why in the world did you have to bring that extra suitcase along, Mimi? You know I hate to get bogged down with luggage overload."

"Take it easy, Papa," Mimi said with a sly smile. "We need to have something to carry our souvenirs back in, right?"

"Well, yeah, but as heavy as that bag is already, the only souvenir you can get is a lei!" Papa said.

"Come on, Christina, let's go check out the beach!" yelled Grant.

Mimi spun around and with a stern look, said, "PLEASE USE YOUR INDOOR VOICE, Grant!" The gruff-looking man at the front desk nodded in agreement with a sneer.

"Uh, OK, how about I take my indoor voice outdoors?" Grant asked. "Come on, Christina," he said again, and made a beeline for the door.

As Christina and Grant stopped to look at the kids' pool, a friendly young girl spoke to them. "Did you know," she said, "that Hawaiian King Kamehameha once used this area as his personal playground in the late 1700s, before the hotel was built?"

Christina and Grant turned around to see a Hawaiian girl with beautiful, long dark hair and tanned skin.

"Yeah, and did you know that Shirley Temple was born here?" added a young boy standing beside her.

"No, Kalino, the Shirley Temple cocktail was invented here!" the girl replied, rolling her eyes. "Hi, my name is Haumea and this is my little brother Kalino. What are your names?"

"I'm Christina and this is MY little brother Grant," Christina said. "Pleased to meet you!"

"Are you on vacation, too?" asked Grant.

"No, we live here," said Kalino. "Maybe we could show you around the island. How long will you be here?"

"Not very long," said Christina. "We're leaving tomorrow evening for Maui."

"The island of Maui is beautiful," Haumea said with a smile. "Kalino and I have visited all six of the Hawaiian islands several times with our parents. We can tell you the coolest things to see."

"Hey, I have an idea. Why don't I ask Mimi and Papa if you could come with us?" said Christina.

"I'll ask our parents and let you know. Thanks!" said Haumea. "By the way, watch out for the man at the front desk at your hotel. Every kid I've talked to who has stayed here has said..." Haumea stopped talking to look at her watch. "Whoops," she said, "come on Kalino, it's later than I thought. Sorry, Christina, but we have to go. I promised my dad we would be back 20 minutes ago. Talk to you later!"

Something occurred to Christina a moment later. "Wait, what about the man at the hotel?" she yelled. The kids were already out of earshot.

So Christina was left wondering what in the world they had to "watch out for."

2
LUAU LADIES

Without getting Papa's or Grant's opinion, Christina and Mimi decided the first order of business was to attend a real Hawaiian luau. The beach was decorated with flaming Tiki torches which flickered red and gold, making the ocean waves sparkle. Each luau table was piled high with purple and yellow hibiscus flowers, wooden dishes, and elaborate centerpieces made from bamboo.

"Look, there are men in girly skirts and necklaces!" Grant said, giggling.

"Those aren't girls' skirts, silly," said Christina. "They're hula skirts, which are part of the costume used to perform traditional Hawaiian dance to music. The flower necklaces are called leis. They are made by sewing tropical flowers to a delicate type of rope."

Grant was about to speak, when all of a sudden he turned and came eye to eye with an enormous dead pig stretched out on a wooden platter. A fat, red apple was stuffed in its mouth, with a pink and purple lei around its neck.

"Why would they try to feed that poor dead pig?" Grant asked.

"They're not feeding him, Grant—he's our dinner!" Papa said. "They cook him in the pit over there for several hours until the meat is as tender as can be. I can't wait to dig in!"

"I still don't understand why they didn't feed him BEFORE he died!" Grant argued.

While Mimi and Papa learned to hula dance, Christina and Grant explored the beach. The night air was filled with the smell of bougainvillea—and smoked pig.

As they walked barefoot in the surf, Christina spied the shadow of someone hiding behind a couple of towering palm trees. All of a sudden, the figure jumped out from behind the trees. Without hesitation, she yelled, "RUN!" and Grant quickly followed. Whoever was hiding was now running after them. Christina looked behind as she ran and noticed a second figure had joined the chase.

"Faster!" she pleaded.

They turned away from the beach and ran toward another hotel, hoping to evade their followers. Suddenly they heard someone scream, "Christina, stop!" When Christina turned to look, she was immediately relieved. "You scared us half to death, Haumea!" Grant said, as he tried to catch his breath.

"You guys ran so fast we couldn't catch up to let you know it was just me and Kalino," Haumea said. She slung her arm around Christina's shoulder. "Hey," she said, "I know a little shop about two minutes from here that sells the sweetest pineapple juice on the island. You two could probably use a cold drink after that run!"

"We're in!" Christina said, still gasping for breath.

As the kids headed on down the beach, they failed to notice more palms, more shadows, and more suspicious eyes watching them.

3
MANGOS AND MYSTERY

Grant awoke in a cold sweat after dreaming that King Kamehameha had been chasing him through the lobby of the "pink potty," his new nickname for the hotel. He noticed that Mimi and Papa were still asleep, so he nudged Christina and told her about his dream.

"He was big and scary and he was throwing coconuts as I ran down the beach," said Grant, his wily hair sticking up all over his head.

"Don't worry, little brother," Christina said, yawning. "It was just your mind mixing all of the things you learned yesterday with the chase from last night."

"I guess you're right," said Grant. "Thanks."

This was their last day on Oahu and they both wanted to make the most of it. As they opened the hotel room door to leave, Christina noticed a coconut in front of the door. A note stuck out of a hole drilled in the top.

"D-d-did you order room service, Christina?" Grant asked nervously.

Without replying, Christina grabbed the note from the coconut and Grant's arm and said, "Follow me!"

They took a seat in the outdoor snack area and read the note:

> 30 YEARS IS MUCH
> TOO LONG, ONLY
> 21 REMAIN STILL
> GOING STRONG

"What does it mean, Christina?" Grant asked.

"I don't know, but you know I'll find out," his sister answered.

"I'm really scared," said Grant. "Should we tell Mimi and Papa?"

"No," Christina said. "There is no need to get them all riled up."

They finished their mango and yogurt and walked to the front desk of the hotel, where the man that Haumea tried to warn them about was working.

"May I help you?" he said with a scowl.

"Yes, sir," Christina started to reply, when she noticed the name on his lapel pin: K. Kamehameha. Trying not to appear spooked, Christina said, "Uh, how long have you been working at the Royal Hawaiian, sir?"

Mr. Kamehameha leaned in with a furrowed brow. "Thirty years. Why do you ask?"

"Just wanted to know how well the hotel retains good people! Bye!" Christina said, and off they ran.

"What was that all about?" Grant asked.

"Nothing," Christina said, hoping Grant had not read his lapel pin.

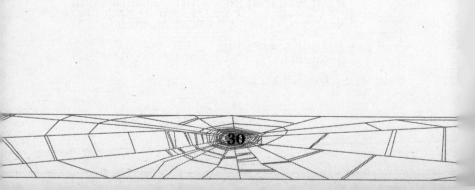

4
SURF, SAND, AND SHARKS

Christina and Grant saw their new friends Haumea and Kalino as they approached the entrance to the hotel.

"Aloha," Haumea said.

"Alohahaha," Grant replied. He was proud of himself that he was able to answer in their native tongue.

"Mahalo," Haumea answered.

"You're hollow? I don't understand," said Grant. His pride quickly vanished.

"I have a free bus pass that will take us all around the island if you'd like to join us," Haumea offered.

"What are we waiting for?" Christina said eagerly. "Let's go!"

Grant looked out the window and exclaimed, "Look, Christina, isn't that Diamond Face?"

"It's Diamond HEAD, not face!" said Christina.

"Whatever," Grant said with a shrug.

As the bus drove north along the coast of Oahu, Christina shared the note that they had found back at the hotel earlier. Neither Haumea nor Kalino had any idea what the clue meant.

"Maybe they left it at the wrong door," Kalino said.

"I guess that's possible," Christina replied. Deep down, she knew it was a mystery she needed to solve.

Christina had never seen roadways that were so dangerously close to the water, as the bus made its way through small beach villages like Makaha and Keaau. The mountainous ranges on the left side of the bus were covered in lavish **flora** and fauna. It reminded her of the movie King Kong and his tropical hideaway jungle.

"Some of these homes are literally *in* the water," Christina exclaimed with surprise. "The landscape here is like being in a different country, compared to the modern, high-rise buildings of downtown Honolulu!"

The bus soon arrived at Waimea Bay Beach. Kalino said, "Let's get off here. I would love to show Grant what real surfing is!" The air was cool and damp. Christina could identify the sweet smell of plumeria as the waves crashed loudly on the reefs.

"The North Shore has some of the best surfing waves in the world," Kalino proudly boasted. "Let's go hang ten!"

"Hang ten what?" Grant asked.

"Just follow me and you'll see!" said Kalino.

Kalino grabbed a couple of boogie boards and gave Grant a brief lesson on how to ride the small waves close to the beach near the famous Banzai Pipeline.

"What's the Banzai Pipeline?" Grant asked.

"Just one of the most famous surfing spots in the world!" Kalino said. "Remember, wait until the wave starts to break before you stand up," he cried above the crash of waves.

Grant watched as the wave approached and his eyes widened when he realized just how big it was. He tried to stand up on the board, but the next thing he knew, he was underwater! He started swimming, but a second wave washed over him and he went under again. As he came up for air, he caught a glimpse of something coming directly at him. He had seen sharks at the aquarium before, and the fin-shaped object headed directly for him looked a lot like what he hoped it was not!

The next thing Grant knew, he was laying on the beach with Christina, Haumea, and Kalino standing over him.

"Grant, Grant, can you hear me?" Christina pleaded.

Grant spoke slowly. "I don't want to know what he chewed off. Just tell me I'm going to live."

"Surfboards don't chew," Kalino replied. "You were hit on the head by a surfboard! I think you'll make it."

Everyone had a good laugh—until a half-chewed coconut washed up on shore next to Grant.

"Those look like "Jaws" teeth marks to me," Grant said.

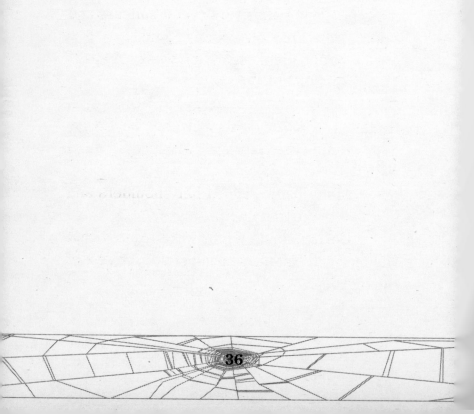

5
VOLCANIC VACATION

As he began to load the plane the next morning, Papa lifted the souvenir suitcase and said, "Mimi, I'm right proud of you!"

"Proud of me for what, Papa?" Mimi replied.

"Proud that you didn't buy anything in Honolulu," he said. "As a matter of fact I'd say the souvenir case feels lighter than it did when we left!"

Mimi just shrugged her shoulders and boarded the *Mystery Girl*.

Christina and Grant were excited that Haumea and Kalino came along for the rest of the journey.

"I can't wait to get to the Big Island," Grant said with excitement. "I hope we get to see some hot guava flowing at Volcanoes National Park!"

"It's called lava, Grant," Christina said, correcting him.

All of a sudden, the *Mystery Girl* lost **altitude** for a brief moment, leaving everyone with the feeling that their stomachs were on the ceiling. "Whew, that was quite the air pocket!" Papa said. "Y'all better recheck your seat belts. We could be in for a bumpy ride." Papa moved the plane to a lower altitude and the ride became smoother.

Christina looked out the window as they began their initial approach to the Big Island of Hawaii and noticed some billowing smoke rising from the ground below. "That must be coming from one of the active volcanoes," she said.

"Yes, that is Kilauea, one of the most active volcanoes in the world," replied Haumea. "Kilauea is the home of Pele, the Hawaiian volcano goddess."

Kalino leaned over to Grant and said, "I'll bet she gets pretty hot in there!" Grant giggled.

Later that morning, Christina, Grant, Haumea, and Kalino boarded a tour van that would take them on their long awaited trip to Hawaii Volcanoes National Park. Christina watched with great interest as the landscape changed dramatically along the way. What looked like ranchland where cows might graze soon became damp rainforest, with moss-covered canopy trees blocking the sunlight.

When they arrived at the summit of Kilauea, Grant heard and smelled something that was not familiar to him. When he looked down, he saw vapor escaping from the ground. "Watch out! It looks like this place is about to blow!"

"Don't worry, Grant," replied Kalino, "it's just a steam vent. You'll see them everywhere on Kilauea."

As Haumea, Grant, and Kalino looked for other vents, Christina walked off in the opposite direction. She glanced to her left and saw a gaping vent spewing ash and rock.

All of a sudden, hot, red molten lava began to flow from the vent. Christina shrieked and turned to run. The lava continued to flow in her direction and appeared to pick up speed. Her heart raced as she ran as fast as she could. She could feel the heat increase through her sneakers. She wondered, could this be the end? At the last moment, Christina darted right and jumped behind a lava rock formation. The molten lava continued on its path and she breathed a momentary sigh of relief.

As she brushed herself off, Christina realized that she had lost track of Grant and their friends. She yelled for them repeatedly, but heard nothing in reply.

Even though she had lost her sense of direction, Christina began to run frantically in the direction she believed would lead her back to the other kids. When she briefly looked back to make sure the lava was not following her, she suddenly tripped over what she thought was a rock. It was not a rock at all...

6
WOWIE, IT'S MAUI!

Christina felt a shiver run through her when she picked up the item that caused her to trip. It was another coconut! Although it was not actually hot to the touch, the coconut was still steaming. What she saw appeared to be a simple math equation burnt into the side of the coconut that read, 4-3=1.

As panic began to set in, Christina heard Grant's voice booming behind her.

"Where have you been?" he asked. "We saw the coolest steaming vents ever. I'll bet nobody has ever been as close as we were to the danger zone!"

Christina exhaled a big sigh of relief. With an exhausted smile, she replied, "Probably not, little brother, probably not."

As the *Mystery Girl* soared over the ocean on their way to Maui, Haumea explained a bit more about the islands. "Hawaii is an isolated archipelago, which means a group of islands. We have the longest island chain in the whole world! There are a great many islands and atolls that make up Hawaii, but there are only six main islands. Besides the two we have already visited—Oahu and the Big Island—Kauai, Lanai, Molokai, and Maui are the others. Maui is my favorite!"

Riding along in the spacious, roofless passenger van, Christina noticed once again how unique and different the island of Maui was from the others. It was immediately obvious to her that this island was sparsely populated compared to the "big city" feel of some areas of Oahu.

"Maui has an abundance of uninhabited land," said Haumea. "Farmland is plentiful and you can find everything from sweet onions to multi-colored protea, a flower with leathery leaves and bursting petals, on the island."

Christina noticed the delicious aroma of pineapples wafting through the air as they passed mile after mile of pineapple groves. Acres of tall sugarcane grass seemed to dance to the force of the gentle tropical breeze.

The van finally stopped in front of a pastel blue cottage on Lahaina Beach, on the northwest coast of the island. Mimi stretched her arms out toward the water and said, "At last, my writer's paradise! Papa, would you be a sweetheart and brew us up a pot of that wonderful Kona coffee? I feel the urge to be creative!"

After a snack of macadamia nuts, the kids quickly put on their bathing suits. They hurried off to the palm-fringed, white-sand beach.

"Who'd like to go snorkeling?" Haumea asked. Three hands jumped into the air and off they went.

Peering through his mask, Grant's blue eyes grew wide at the vibrant turquoise, orange, and yellow tropical fish hovering near the ocean floor. They promptly scattered as he approached. As he dove to get a closer look, a thick, purple-striped Moray eel lunged at his mask! Grant flipped backwards to avoid the eel, landing on a sharp, whitish object.

"Wow," he gasped. "You're coming with me!" Grant grabbed his treasure and struggled to lug it back to the beach.

"Look what I found," he said. "It's an elephant tusk!"

Christina examined the curious object and said, "This isn't an elephant tusk. It's scrimshaw."

"What's scrimshaw?" Grant asked.

"Scrimshaw's an art form that whalers made famous in the 1800s," Haumea explained. "During long, lonesome hours at sea, they often etched words and pictures on the bones of sperm whales."

As Christina studied it more closely, her eyes opened wide and the others looked at her curiously. She showed them the problem. One side of the scrimshaw had a perfectly etched replica of a map of Maui, while the other had the word:

DANGER

They were in over their heads. It was time to tell Papa.

7
CUCKOO FOR COCONUTS

Mimi and Papa were enjoying the laid-back pace of Maui. For Mimi, the warm sun and solitude of the cottage's back porch seemed to release a thousand ideas for possible chapters for her book. "It should always be this easy," she thought to herself. "They seem to be writing themselves!"

Just then, Papa joined her on the porch and said, "I'm gonna go hunting, Mimi."

"Hunting?" Mimi had never known Papa to hunt for anything but his lost car keys. "Hunt for what, pray tell?"

"Seashells! What else?" Papa replied as he bounded off the porch, laughing.

Ever since he was a young boy, Papa had always been interested in seashells. He found the variety of sizes, shapes, and colors fascinating. He also loved the fact that they can be found on beaches all over the world. He'd built up quite a collection that Christina and Grant liked to borrow for Show and Tell at school.

Papa strolled along Lahaina for a couple of miles, stopping frequently to collect shells that caught his eye. He found brown-spotted igloo shells, orange and yellow spiral shells, and a variety of interesting snail shells, which he rinsed off in the clear, blue-green water before placing them in his canvas bag. "Can't wait to show the kids the new additions to the collection," he thought as he made his way back.

Papa was about a quarter mile from the cottage when he noticed the kids running toward him, frantically waving their arms to get his attention.

"Papa, Papa!" Christina yelled as she approached.

"What's wrong, young lady?" Papa

asked, curious.

"We're in great danger!" Christina answered. "Several creepy things have happened since we got to Hawaii and we found some things with scary messages. I thought I could handle it all myself, b-b-but the last one was too much," she said, handing him a bag containing the coconut clues.

"Why, these aren't anything to be afraid of," Papa said with a hearty laugh. "Hey, wait a minute! Are you kids trying to play a trick on me?" he asked, smiling.

"No," shouted Grant. "Here, look at this!"

Papa looked at the scrimshaw and immediately realized that the kids couldn't have created something this **ornate**, joking or not. As he studied it more closely, Papa noticed that the style of the lettering on all of the clues was very similar. He was now convinced that he needed to take the warning on the etched whalebone seriously.

Mimi was still working on her manuscript when Papa and the kids returned to the cottage. "How was everyone's day?"

Mimi inquired.

"Let's go have a seat in the living room. We need to talk," Papa answered. Mimi could tell by the look on his face and the tone of his voice that he was tense and worried about something.

As Mimi listened intently, Christina and Grant explained all of the strange things that had occurred since they'd arrived in Hawaii. Mimi looked at the message from the Royal Hawaiian, all of the coconuts, and the scrimshaw.

"Papa, I don't like the sound of this," Mimi said. "We need to pack and leave for the airport immediately!"

"But we came to Maui so you could write in peace," Papa replied. "What about your book?"

"The book will have to wait," Mimi insisted. "We're leaving tonight!"

While Christina was relieved, she was disappointed that they would not be able to spend more time in Maui. After she finished packing her bag, she decided to wait outside for the van. As Christina opened the door, she saw something fall from the roof. She jumped out of the way as it crashed on the steps. It was another coconut! Christina bent down, picked it up, and read the freshly painted message:

MOLOKAI OR
GOODBYE!

8
NO STOPS, JUST GO

The *Mystery Girl* rumbled down the dark runway, picking up speed as Papa lifted off for Molokai. Rain began to streak the plane's windows like tears. As they gained altitude, lightning suddenly filled the sky, followed by a BOOM, the loudest thunderclap strike anyone aboard had ever heard! The plane's interior lights flickered, then went out, leaving it pitch black inside the cabin.

"I'm afraid of the dark!" shrieked Kalino.

"Don't worry, it'll be OK," said Papa. "We'll give it a few minutes until the electrical storm passes and I'll reset the lighting system."

"Tell everyone about Molokai, Kalino," Haumea suggested to help take his mind off the dark. "He knows *everything* about that island," she continued in an encouraging voice.

"Well," Kalino began, "Molokai is an interesting place. The most famous person ever to live on the island was a priest called Father Damien. In 1873, he volunteered to serve at the Kalawao leprosy colony, even though the disease was considered highly contagious at that time. Father Damien built homes and hospitals and nursed patients without fear for his own safety. He was a truly great man!"

"What is leprosy?" asked Grant.

"It's a disease," Kalino explained. "It can cause a lot of damage to people's faces and skin. They might even lose a nose or fingers. Sometimes, people are afraid of them or make fun of them, but Father Damien just saw them as ordinary people stricken by a terrible disease."

The children were quiet, trying to imagine such a life.

"There are also no stop lights on the island!" Haumea said, to change the subject.

"Wow!" said Grant. "That means we can go, go, go!"

The storm soon passed and Papa was able to get the lights back on, just in time for a smooth landing on Molokai.

"I called ahead and rented a four-wheel drive vehicle and a tent," said Mimi. "So we'll leave most of our baggage on the Mystery Girl while we camp."

Papa chimed in and told them that they would be hiking Halawa Valley the next day. "The first Polynesian settlers made Halawa Valley their home," he said.

Haumea leaned over to Christina and whispered, "There are ruins of ancient temples in Halawa. Two of them are famous because human sacrifices were performed there!"

"Great," groused Christina. "Human sacrifices and a dreaded disease...sounds like we're out of the frying pan into the fire."

The road to Halawa was not paved and the soil was deep red in color. The vehicle did not provide a smooth ride, but the scenery more than made up for it. Papa stopped the vehicle at an overlook and said, "Come with me, everyone. This is what I call a magnificent sight!"

Looking through the fine mountain mist, Christina could see the shoreline more than 700 feet below where they stood. The lush, green mountainside ended abruptly in white, foamy waves lapping at the shoreline. The sparkling blue ocean stretched as far as the kids could see.

"This is really breathtaking, Papa. Thanks for stopping!" Christina said.

"I don't know about you, Kalino, but I still have my breath!" Grant joked.

"Yeah, and it doesn't smell good, either," Christina teased back.

They drove for a while longer, then stopped to pitch their tent.

Oh, well, thought Christina, as she snuggled down into her sleeping bag. What could go too far wrong in paradise, anyway?

The next morning, Kalino woke Christina, Grant, and Haumea just as the sun peeked through the thick, pulpy leaves of the Naupaka shrubs. Christina wanted to pick a few of the white and purple streaked flowers because their petals only grew on the bottom. That's so odd, she thought, it looks like half a flower!

"I want you to see Moaula Falls, guys," Kalino said. "It's a beautiful place and legend has it that there is a giant lizard in the pool at the bottom of the falls!"

The kids followed the path of a sparkling stream, which led them to the massive waterfall. The roar of the falls got louder as they got closer, when suddenly it appeared out of the green, plush trees of the forest. The water plunged down with tremendous force and they could feel its mist dancing on their skin.

"Let's go for a swim in the natural pool," yelled Grant, and the others gladly followed. He knew Mimi counted any swim as their "bath" for the day, which was perfectly all right with him.

"It's tradition to throw a leaf in the water before you swim," said Kalino. "If it floats, you're safe. If it sinks, it means the lizard is waiting for you!"

Grant threw his leaf into the water and dove right in behind it.

"Guess he doesn't believe in legends," Haumea said.

They swam and played in the pool, dunking their heads beneath the water from the falls. Christina turned to tell Grant that it was probably time to start back, but couldn't find him. Kalino had vanished as well. Christina searched the area where they had jumped in, but the boys weren't there either. Haumea pointed toward the water.

"What's wrong?" Christina asked.

"There are only two leaves floating in the pool," Haumea answered, with a look of terror. "Only yours and mine!"

9
LIZARD LAIR

Christina and Haumea realized that they had to act quickly if they were going to find the boys.

"Let's split up and check the whole area around the pool," Christina said. "Meet me back here in 30 minutes."

"Sounds good," Haumea said, scampering off.

Christina dove back into the water and began searching underwater for the boys. She couldn't see much. The thick trees of the rainforest acted as a shield, blocking out most of the sunlight.

As she came up for air on the north side of the waterfall pool, Christina spied a small, red and white lizard perched on a rock. She picked it up and said, "Please tell me that you are the real lizard the legend was based on!" The lizard just squiggled out of her hand. Christina returned to the water to continue her search.

Haumea swam under the flowing water until she was directly behind the falls. She called for Kalino and Grant, but heard nothing in return. As she sat on the ground trying to think of where the boys might have gone, Haumea saw something bobbing in the water. As the object floated toward her, she noticed it was a coconut, cracked evenly down the middle. When Haumea picked it up it broke into two perfect halves. She turned one piece over and saw a message:

SACRIFICE

Haumea quickly studied the other half, which said:

TONIGHT

"Christina!" she screamed as loudly as she could.

Christina arrived a moment later, out of breath from her underwater search. "Did you find anything?" she asked, not completely sure that she wanted to hear the answer.

"Look at these," Haumea said, handing the coconut halves to Christina.

"I don't understand," Christina started to say, when she suddenly remembered what Haumea had told her earlier about the ancient temples. "We need to get to the temple ruins as soon as we can! Do you know how to get there?"

Haumea reached into her waterproof fanny pack and pulled out a map of Molokai.

"We are currently here," Haumea said, pointing to the map. "It looks like if we walk about a mile or so west, we should arrive at the ruins."

"Let's ROLL!" Christina said with urgency.

Walking through the rainforest was difficult. A snarl of tangled tree roots hidden under the thick brush of strawberry guava trees made it tough for the girls not to trip and fall along the way. As difficult as the terrain was to navigate, the bright red flowers of the Ohia tree and other tropical vegetation continued to remind Christina of just how beautiful the Hawaiian Islands are.

"I don't know if I can go another step," said Haumea. She plopped down on the ground in exhaustion.

"We have to keep moving," Christina replied. "It'll be dark soon and we won't be able to get back to camp."

Christina took a step forward, but caught her foot in a maze of brush. She pulled hard, but only fell forward.

"Help, Haumea, my foot is trapped!" Christina pleaded.

Christina reached into her backpack and pulled out the pocketknife that Papa had given her as a present before they left.

"Use the jagged-edged blade if you need to cut through something thick," she recalled Papa saying.

Christina started sawing away at the small, but strong branches, which broke away one by one, until she freed herself.

It was now dark, and there was no chance that Christina and Haumea would make it back to camp that night. They found a small opening to what looked like a cave and decided to stay there for the night.

"This will keep us dry if it rains and safe from any predators that may be in the forest," Christina said. "Hopefully."

The girls made makeshift cots from large leaves and flowers and tried to sleep until sunrise. What they did not realize was the fact that they were sleeping in one of the temple ruins—one of the two where human sacrifices occurred regularly years ago!

Even though she was sleeping on a bed of leaves, Christina was resting comfortably. She stirred slightly, rubbed her eyes, then turned over the other way to go back to sleep. As she did, Christina caught a glimpse of what appeared to be light.

Her eyes flew open in shock. There were Grant and Kalino tied to a gigantic bamboo altar, surrounded by tiki torches! Standing in front of the altar was the biggest human figure Christina had ever seen. He had long, dark hair, and a menacing look on his face. A lei made of bones hung around his thick neck.

The man turned to face the altar. Raising his burly arms to the sky, he cried in a booming voice, "Pele, Goddess of Fire, it is I, Kamehameha. I humbly offer these young humans as a sacrifice for all, who have denied your power and greatness!"

As Kamehameha touched a torch to the bed of dry grass beneath Grant's and Kalino's feet, Christina felt someone grab her from behind and everything went dark.

"Christina, wake up, wake up!"

It was Haumea gently shaking Christina by the shoulders.

"You must have had a terribly bad dream!" Haumea said.

Christina looked around and realized it was morning. The scary experience with Kamehameha had just been a horrible nightmare. She was very relieved.

"I dreamed that King Kamehameha was getting ready to sacrifice the boys for Pele," Christina said. "It was awful!"

"I wasn't able to sleep at all," said Haumea. "I was awake all night and there has been nobody here except you and me."

Christina sighed when she remembered that meant the boys were still missing.

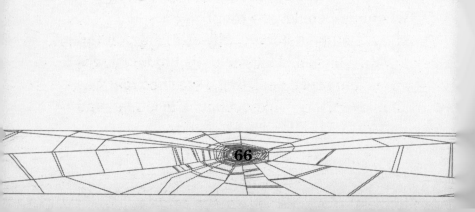

10
RAUCOUS RUINS

Christina and Haumea took one more look around the waterfall before they decided it was time to go and tell Mimi and Papa what had happened. It was noon by the time they reached the tent. Christina hurriedly opened the tent flap, but found nobody there. She ran outside to see if their rented vehicle was there, but it was gone too!

"First, Grant and Kalino disappear, and now Mimi and Papa are gone," Christina said. What more could go wrong?

Haumea stood eerily still and pointed toward a jagged black rock. Painted on it was an ancient scene depicting a sacrifice that was almost exactly like what Christina had described from her dream, with one exception—two boys and two adults were tied to the altar!

The girls ran as fast as they could back toward the ruins. After about five minutes, they heard a vehicle approaching and turned to see if it was Papa. What they saw was a park ranger driving a green Jeep. As it came to a stop, the woman called out to the girls, "Aloha, my name is Alani. Is everything OK here?"

"Thank goodness you're here," Christina shouted. "Things are not OK and we could really use your help!"

Christina and Haumea told the ranger all about what had happened over the past 24 hours. They also explained that Mimi and Papa were not at the tent site when they returned.

"Jump in, girls, I'll help you solve this mystery," the ranger said.

Alani drove as fast as she could on the bumpy terrain back toward the waterfall. When they arrived, Christina and Haumea led her to the spot where they had last seen the boys.

"Do you think the giant lizard may have taken them?" Haumea asked Alani.

"No, sweetheart, that is just a nasty old legend," Alani said. "I've been working this area for 20 years and have swum in this pool hundreds of times. Never seen anything bigger than a chameleon in all that time!"

Christina felt a bit more at ease, but was still concerned about the painting on the rock. "Can we go back to the ruins and look for them one more time?" she asked.

"Certainly, hop in," Alani said.

They arrived at the site of the ruins and Alani followed them into the hidden cave where they had slept the night before.

"This is where I had the dream about Kamehameha sacrificing Grant and Kalino," said Christina.

Alani looked around and smiled. "Sometimes dreams can seem so real that we start to believe they are real. I can assure you that human sacrifices have not occurred here for many, many years."

"Wait a minute," Haumea interrupted. "Then how do you explain the rock painting?"

"Rock painting?" Alani asked.

"Yes, when we got back to the campsite there was a painting showing Kamehameha getting ready to sacrifice Grant, Kalino, Mimi, and Papa," Christina explained.

Alani was confident that the girls' imaginations were working overtime, but she wanted to see for herself. "Come on, I'll drive you back to the tent so we can get to the bottom of this."

When they arrived, Papa was standing outside, breaking down the tent. Hearing the Jeep pull up, Papa turned around and said, "Where in the world have you two been? Mimi and I have been worried sick about you!"

"Papa, I am so sorry," Christina said. "I know I should have watched Grant more closely! But I didn't know that there was a giant lizard living at the bottom of the waterfall and I didn't want to put you and Mimi in harm's way and I..."

"Slow down there, darlin'! What in the heck are you babbling on about?" Papa asked. "Grant and Kalino got back just before nightfall yesterday. They are with Mimi and Kalino's father Kano, back on the Big Island. He called yesterday and asked if he could bring Grant along on a trip to visit Keck Observatory. We thought you would be back shortly after, so I stayed behind and told them we'd meet them there."

"How did they get back to the Big Island?" Christina asked.

"Um, Papa's not the only one with his own plane, Christina," Haumea said. "Dad has one as well. He calls it *Makani*, which means 'the wind'."

"It looks like my work here is done," Alani said. "By the way, before I leave, can I see that painted rock you told me about?"

"Sure," said Christina. "It's right over..." Looking at the rock, she saw that there was no painting on it at all. "But I swear on my Girl Scout's honor that there was a painting," Christina insisted, looking over at Haumea.

"I saw it, too," Haumea added. "But with all that has happened, I can't be sure of anything anymore."

"Well, I know one thing. You two have the most vivid imaginations I've ever seen!" Papa said. "Even more than Mimi, and that's saying a lot. Now let's finish breaking down the tent so we can catch up with the others on the Big Island!"

Big Island, Christina thought. Does that mean more Big Mystery?

11
WHAT THE KECK?

Kano drove the four-wheel drive vehicle steadily along the steep, unpaved road, masterfully navigating the challenging terrain. He, Grant, and Kalino were making their way to visit the Keck Observatory. It is located at the summit of Mauna Kea, the highest point in Hawaii and the Pacific Basin.

"It seems like we're heading for the moon!" Grant said. "How far up do we have to go before we reach Keck Observatory?"

"The observatory is on the summit of Mauna Kea, which is almost 14,000 feet above sea level," Kano replied. "If you measure it from its base, Mauna Kea is the tallest mountain on Earth, at more than 30,000 feet!"

"Wow!" Grant exclaimed. "Never mind the moon, we're on our way to Mars! Too bad Mimi stayed behind at the hotel. I would never miss an adventure like this because I wanted to write some silly book."

"Your grandmother's writing is the reason you get to experience these great adventures," Kano reminded him.

"You're right," Grant said. "Sorry, Mimi, wherever you are."

Although Kano now held the position of superintendent of the *USS Arizona* Memorial, he had studied astronomy at the University of California, which is one of only seven communities allowed to have observing time at Keck. Grant felt lucky to have found a friend whose dad was so well connected.

Kano pulled into a parking lot with a sign that read: Welcome to Onizuka Visitor Station. Before they got out of the vehicle, Kano gave the boys some instructions.

"Mauna Kea is one of the places in the world where you can drive from sea level to an altitude of almost 14,000 feet in about two hours," Kano said. "At that altitude, there's approximately 40 percent less oxygen in the air, which can lead to altitude sickness. We'll need to stay here for at least 30 minutes until our bodies adjust to the new altitude."

After the stop at the visitor's center, they drove a short distance and stopped again. Grant saw a sign that indicated they were now at 11,000 feet.

"Only 3,000 more feet to go!" Grant said with excitement.

Kano pulled over and parked again. "Welcome to Hawaii's highest National Historical Landmark—the Mauna Kea adze quarry," Kano said.

"I don't see anything but a pile of rocks," Grant said.

"You're right, Grant," Kano replied, "but it's the type of rock that's interesting. This quarry covers approximately eight square miles and is the only one of its kind in the United States." Reaching down to pick up a rock, Kano explained, "This fine-grained, dense stone is called basalt. It's actually harder than some types of steel."

"Cool, but what is an adze?" Grant asked.

"An adze is an old-fashioned woodworking tool, very similar to an ax," Kano answered.

"Hey, I wonder if George Washington used an adze to chop down the cherry tree," Grant said with a sly smile.

"Sounds like you and Kalino will get along just fine!" Kano said, grinning.

Grant closely studied the landscape on the remainder of the drive to the Keck Observatory. He noticed the contrast of red rock and black rock cylinder cones created by volcanic activity. As they approached the summit, Grant noticed what looked like two gigantic golf balls.

"What are those?" Grant inquired.

"Those are the twin Keck Telescopes," Kalino said.

"They still look like giant golf balls to me!" said Grant.

With Papa at the controls of the *Mystery Girl*, Christina and Haumea finally felt at ease. The girls slept peacefully all the way to the Big Island. Christina awoke to the sound of the landing gear adjusting for landing.

"Are we here already?" she said in amazement.

"Yes, siree!" Papa replied. "You two have been in dreamland since we left Molokai."

"I guess I was more tired than I thought!" Christina said.

Grant was intently listening to their private tour guide explain the history of the observatory when Papa and the girls entered the room.

"Papa! Christina!" Grant shouted. "Boy, have I missed you guys!"

"We missed you too, Grant," Christina replied. "I thought you were—oh, never mind—at least we're all together again. Wait a minute, where's Mimi?" Christina asked, looking all around.

"Aloha, I'm Kano, Kalino and Haumea's father," Kano said. "Your grandmother stayed behind to catch up on her manuscript. She's staying at a hotel on Hilo Bay and we'll meet her there afterward."

"Hi, Kano, I'm Papa, the cowboy pilot of the *Mystery Girl*," Papa said as he shook Kano's hand. "Thank you for taking good care of Grant while I was corralling the young ladies."

"My pleasure," Kano replied. "If you will excuse me, I have a brief meeting to attend with one of the scientists. Can you drive the kids back to the hotel?"

"No problem; we'll see you later," Papa replied. "I'm sure you've got stars and planets to wrangle!"

Papa and the kids continued the tour. "Our twin telescopes are the largest optical and infrared telescopes in the world," the tour guide said. "Each telescope stands eight stories tall and weighs 300 tons, which is the equivalent weight of fifty 12,000-pound elephants!"

"WOW, that's a lot of trunks! How far can you see with the telescope?" Grant asked.

"These scopes will bring objects that are more than 10 billion light years away into view," the tour guide answered.

"How many miles is that?" Grant inquired.

"One light year is equal to about 6 trillion miles," said the guide.

"Trying to figure that out will give me more of a headache than any old altitude sickness!" Grant said.

Papa thanked their tour guide and herded the kids toward the exit. Christina climbed into the back seat of the vehicle and sat down.

"What the..." she said.

She reached behind her and found a miniature ax.

"Look! The last person who rented this truck must have forgotten to take their souvenir ax home with them," Christina said.

"Let me see that," said Kalino. "That's not an ax, it's an ancient adze, and look, there's writing on the handle." The words said:

> THIS ISLAND IS HAUNTED, RIGHT TO THE CORE; RETURN TO OAHU, WHERE YOU'LL SOON FIND OUT MORE.

Christina handed the new clue to Papa, who scratched his chin and said, "We need to get back and find Mimi as soon as possible!"

12
ALL FOR ONE

After a 45-minute drive, Papa and the kids arrived at The Inn at Kulaniapia Falls in Hilo, where Mimi was staying. Christina and Grant immediately fell in love with the surroundings of the inn and could not wait to explore.

A lovely, young Hawaiian woman approached them and said, "Welcome! May I help you?"

"Yes, thank you," Papa answered. "I need these bags taken to Carole Marsh's room, please. And would you let her know that Papa and the kids have arrived?"

"It would be my pleasure, sir," the woman said. "Ms. Marsh is staying in the

Pagoda Guest House. Leave your bags here and I will arrange to have them brought to you. Follow me."

The Pagoda Guest House was a three-story private residence built on a cliff that overlooked Kulaniapia Falls.

"Is that who I think it is?" Mimi shouted with joy in her voice. "Let me turn off this computer and I'll be right down."

Grant and Christina couldn't wait to see her and bounded up the stairs.

"Mimi," Grant cried, as he threw his arms around her. "I was beginning to think I'd never see you again!"

"Tell me all about your adventures," Mimi said, as both children held onto one arm each.

Papa, Kalino, and Haumea chimed in as Christina and Grant shared their experiences with Mimi.

"I had no idea you kids were lost, but thank goodness you weren't in any kind of serious danger," Mimi said.

"Not in danger?!" Christina replied in shock. "Then what do you call sleeping in a cave and the risk of being sacrificed?"

"An adventure followed by a most imaginative dream!" Mimi said. "You may have read one too many mysteries!"

Sensing their frustration, Papa spoke up in Christina's defense. "Christina and Haumea were lost in the jungle, Mimi. Spending the night in a cave can be quite terrifying, even for an adult! I'm getting a bit uncomfortable myself," Papa confided, as he pulled the adze out of his pocket. "What do you make of this?" He handed the adze to Mimi.

Mimi studied the artifact and asked for one of the coconuts. "The lettering is consistent on all of these clues," she said. "I didn't mean to make fun of your feelings. I can now understand why you're concerned!"

"Well, it's about time you got on board, woman," Papa said in a pretend scolding voice. "We can't all just sit around and write about the fantasy world. Some of us *live* it!"

"What will we do next?" Grant asked with anticipation.

"Papa, I think we'll be safe here for another day or two," Mimi said. "Why don't you relax at the spa while I finish the next few chapters of my book? I'm at a critical point in the story and don't want to lose my momentum."

"OK," Papa answered. "But as soon as you're done with those chapters, we're heading back to Oahu to get to the bottom of whatever this mess is! You kids need to stay on the inn property until we leave—no exceptions!"

"Don't worry about us, Papa," Grant said confidently. "We can take care of ourselves!"

"Speak for yourself, little brother," said Christina. "Personally, I think the four of us need to stick together. After all, anything could happen—and often does to us!"

13
HILO HIJINKS

Christina awakened to the now familiar sound of the waterfall. She quietly woke the other children, trying not to disturb Mimi and Papa.

"Let's eat," Grant said, "I'm starving!"

The children walked downstairs to the kitchen and found an appetizing display of tropical fruit, a tray of baked muffins, and two pitchers of freshly squeezed papaya and mango juice.

"This will work!" said Kalino.

Haumea began to fill her glass with juice when she noticed an envelope that said, "Please Read."

"I don't want to know what's in there," Haumea said with concern.

Christina grabbed the envelope, carefully opened it, and read it to the others. "'Compliments of management!' It looks like we might be safe here after all!"

Haumea found a brochure that described the layout of the property and its amenities. "Located on 22 lush, tropical acres with our own, private 120-foot-high waterfall, which spills into a deep, crystal clear pool..."

"I wouldn't mind walking around it, but I know I've had enough of waterfalls for one vacation!" said Christina.

"Me, too," added Kalino. "Let's take a walk through the gardens instead."

The children carefully walked along a trail that eventually led to the bottom of the falls. Yellow, orange, pink, and white hibiscus lined the trail. A pleasing scent that Christina and Grant could not identify mixed in with the sweet, floral fragrance.

"What is that smell?" Grant asked.

"That's macadamia," Haumea replied. "We passed many acres of macadamia trees on the way to the inn." She bent down, picked up a green ripened nut from the ground, and showed it to the others.

"Did you know that unripe macadamia nuts are a feral pig's favorite food?" Kalino asked Grant and Christina.

"What's a feral pig?" Christina asked.

"Wild pigs that wander the rainforest," Kalino answered. "Nothing to worry about; they just need to eat like everyone else!"

The children continued to follow the path, when they came to a garden lined with a variety of tall, green bamboo trees. The roar of the waterfall, combined with the gentle rustle of bamboo leaves, made a sound unlike anything Christina had ever heard. This truly is paradise, she thought to herself.

Grant walked over to the edge of the trail, amazed by how thick the bamboo leaves were. He said to the others, "Let's hike into this bamboo forest. I'll bet it's pretty cool!"

"Remember what Papa said," Christina warned. "No exceptions! We don't want to break the rules."

"What he said was to stay on the inn property," Grant said. "The bamboo *is* on the property."

"He's right," said Haumea.

"Alright," Christina said, "but we need to return to the trail when I say so."

"OK, I understand," Grant agreed, fingers crossed behind his back.

The children trudged into the bamboo forest and soon found an open area covered from top to bottom with small, gray, intertwined branches. It was shaped like an igloo, as if custom made for the perfect hideaway.

"I brought some of the leftover fruit from breakfast with me," said Haumea. "Let's have a picnic!"

"Great idea!" the others replied.

As the kids sat and ate pineapples and mangoes, a sudden loud rustling noise startled them. Christina looked intently, but could not see anything. A moment later, they heard it again, only it seemed much closer this time.

"Don't move," Christina whispered, spotting a slowly moving shadow about 10 feet away. "Give me your pocketknife, Grant!"

Christina moved stealthily toward whatever was hiding in the bush, prepared to let out a petrifying scream. Then, she realized the monster in her mind was merely a small piglet munching on a macadamia nut.

"False alarm, guys!" she said with relief.

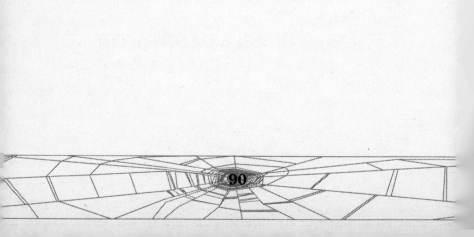

14

AERIAL SAFARI

When the children returned to the Pagoda, Papa was preparing dinner in the kitchen.

"What are you making, Papa?" Christina asked.

"Poke," Papa answered.

"What is po-kay?" asked Grant.

"It's a traditional Hawaiian dish made from the freshest seafood available," Papa explained.

Christina looked at the strange mixture in the bowl and asked, "Do you fry it or broil it?"

"Neither," said Papa. "It marinates in sesame oil, ginger, chile peppers and green onions, and then you eat it!"

"Raw?" said Grant. "I think I would rather have poi!"

"Don't worry, Grant," Mimi said. "That's exactly what we're having for our side dish. I made it fresh this afternoon!"

After dinner, everyone sat outside on the lawn behind the guesthouse to watch the magical Hawaiian sunset.

"This has been the best day of the vacation," Christina said. "Nobody got lost, no threatening clues, *no coconuts!*"

Just as the sun began to set, a car drove up to the guesthouse. It was Kano.

"Daddy!" Haumea and Kalino shouted at the same time.

"I had a free day and thought I would come to check up on you. How have my children been behaving?" Kano asked Mimi and Papa.

"You should be proud," Papa answered. "They are very well mannered."

"Well then, a surprise is in order!" Kano said. "A very dear friend of mine owns a helicopter tour service here on the island. He has offered to take the children on an aerial tour of the volcanoes."

"Grant, you're going to love it!" Kalino squealed. "It's so cool to watch the rivers of lava flowing from up above!"

"I think I might skip this one," Christina said. "I've already had enough close encounters with lava!"

"I have an idea," said Mimi. "How about a girls-only shopping trip while the boys go on the helicopter tour?"

"That's a great idea!" Christina answered. "I want to buy a muumuu and some other Hawaiian clothes."

"Papa, you're invited to go on the tour as well," said Kano.

"Thank you, but I think I'll stay right here and enjoy the solitude," Papa said. "And cook!"

Kano and the boys left early the next morning to get to the helipad for their adventure. When they arrived, Kano's friend Pika was there to greet them.

"Aloha!" Pika said.

"Aloha!" the boys replied.

"Before we take off, I want to show you the helicopter we'll be flying in," said Pika.

Grant looked to his left and saw a blue helicopter with the words *Air Avenger* printed boldly on the side. "Is this it?"

"That's the one!" Pika answered. "It's called an A-STAR 350."

As they took off from the helipad, Grant commented, "Taking off in a helicopter is so different than it is in the *Mystery Girl*!"

Soon, they were flying high over Hilo and with the clear, sunny skies, had an unforgettable view of the Big Island. Grant was impressed that he had his own headset and pretended to be the co-pilot.

"Co-captain to captain," Grant said. "Can you give me our current altitude please, over?"

Grant's enthusiasm reminded Pika of his own childhood dream of flying and he picked up the two-way microphone to play along.

"Current altitude is 1,500 feet, co-captain. Proceeding to Kilauea," Pika replied. Approaching Kilauea, Grant could see lava lakes and beaming skylights. Lava was flowing into the ocean, creating black sand beaches as he watched.

Pika pointed downward. "If you look to the left, you'll see the Lava Tree Forest. Many years ago, a lava flow poured over this patch of wet Ohia trees, leaving behind lava tubes where each one had previously stood."

"Poor trees had no chance," Grant said.

Just before they circled to make their way back to Hilo, the helicopter turned sideways and began to fall straight down toward the middle of the steaming crater.

"Make sure your seatbelts are tight, I can't seem to pull this baby back up!" Pika said loudly over the microphone. "Prepare for a crash landing!"

Grant closed his eyes as tightly as he could, wishing he had gone on the shopping trip with Mimi and Christina. Even muumuus seemed better than falling out of the frying pan of a helicopter into a fire of a volcano. He peeked out of a corner of his eye and saw that Kalino was giggling, with his hand over his mouth. Grant realized he had been the victim of a joke!

"If you expect to be a real pilot someday, you must know what to do in a crisis," Pika said.

"You really got me, guys!" Grant said, but he knew that Papa would never have played such a trick. Were these people his friends, or enemies?

15
SEA SKULLS

"I have great news," said Mimi. "I've completed every chapter of my book except for the finale, which can wait for a couple of days. Y'all have been so patient with me while I've been writing that I planned a surprise for everyone."

"I love a surprise!" Grant said.

"Me, too!" Christina added.

"Me, three!" Papa yelled. "What have you been up to, Mimi?" he asked with a sly smile.

Mimi held up a brochure and announced, "Deep sea fishing!"

"COOOOOOOL!" all of the children replied.

"I hired a fishing boat for the day that will take us out for eight hours of deep sea adventure. It says here that we may even see humpback whales on the journey!" Mimi said.

"I'll bring my video camera just in case we do," Haumea offered.

The clock read 4:30 a.m. when the children's alarm rang.

"Up and at 'em!" Papa shouted. "It's a long drive to the Kona coast. We'll need to leave in 20 minutes to make launch time!"

Papa was looking forward to the excursion more than anyone. As a boy, he loved to read stories about famous sea captains and imagined becoming one himself someday. Captain Cook was one of his favorites and the fact that Cook had discovered Hawaii made the fishing trip even more exciting.

"Did you know that the Captain Cook Monument is close to Kona?" Papa said to Mimi.

"Not only was I aware of it, Papa, I talked the fishing boat captain into heading

south so you would be able to see it!"
Mimi replied.

"Well, shiver me timbers! You're the
greatest wife a sailor could ask for!" Papa said
as he hugged Mimi.

When they arrived in Kona, the *Hoku*
was prepared to head to sea. Four deep-sea
fishing rods were set in steel holders in front
of deck chairs with harnesses. Several red and
white coolers were packed with ice, in
preparation for the day's catch. As they
boarded the boat, an older man with white hair
and leathery skin welcomed them.

"My name is Woody Stevens and I'll be
your captain today," said the man. "Do we
have any seaman recruits with us today?"

"What is a seaman recruit?" Grant
answered.

"Well, if you don't know what it is, then
you probably are one!" Woody said, chuckling.
"Let's get underway, mates!"

The *Hoku* left the dock at 10 a.m. sharp
and headed due south. The aqua water of the
Pacific was calm as it gently splashed against

the sides of the boat. The sun was shining brightly and white, puffy clouds dotted the sky.

"You picked a beautiful day for fishing," Woody said to the group. "Word has it the ahi are running strong today. I need everyone's attention to tell you all about the rules of the ship. First, each person needs to wear his or her lifejacket at all times. Number two, you must wear your harness when fishing. If you hook something, let me know and I'll help you reel it in. Number three, no hanging over the side of the boat. I don't want anyone to become shark bait. Last, but not least, have fun!" added the captain as he made his way back to the helm.

Christina gulped and said, "Shark bait? Have fun? Easy for him to say!"

Grant, Mimi, and Papa stood near the bow, watching dolphins playfully jump as they escorted the boat through the water.

"Look!" Papa said with youthful glee, pointing off the port side of the boat. "There's the Captain Cook monument!"

"Who's Captain Cook?" Grant asked. "How many arms does he have? Does he know Peter Pan?"

"Captain James Cook was a great British explorer who discovered the Hawaiian Islands," Papa answered.

Captain Stevens slowed the engines as they approached and called out, "The water's too shallow for the *Hoku* to get close enough to anchor. If you want to see it up close, you'll need to take our rowboat over."

"No need, Captain, I'm happy just to have been here. Besides, we've got some fishing to do!" Papa said.

Captain Stevens revved the engines and they were off to the deep sea!

After an hour of cruising, Christina noticed that the *Hoku's* engines had shut down. She could not see shoreline in any direction. How peaceful, she thought, just like a real paradise.

"This should be a perfect spot to cast our lines and begin catching us some fish," Captain Stevens shouted. "Man the poles, mates!" he commanded.

Once he had confirmed that everyone was safely harnessed and ready, the captain started the engines and they were off.

"Keep your finger on the line to feel the tension," Papa said to Grant and Christina, who were holding their fishing poles the way the captain had shown them. "When you feel it move, start reeling as fast as you can."

About five minutes passed before Christina shouted, "I think I've got something!"

Papa, an experienced angler, unlocked his harness and hurried over to help Christina reel in her catch.

"Lean the rod forward and pull back as you continue to take up the slack," Papa instructed.

Christina continued to battle for about 15 minutes. All of a sudden, the stern of the boat rose 12 feet in the air and crashed back down violently. Mimi looked up in terror and screamed, "It's a whale!"

The curious creature circled back under the boat and rose again to the surface, tipping the boat harder. Christina saw that Papa was barely hanging on to a rope and decided she had to act quickly. She let go of the reel and swung her chair in Papa's direction, lowering the pole so he could grab hold of it.

Papa was able to grip the pole with his left hand just as the rope snapped in two. As the whale swam away, the boat settled back to an even keel. Papa wrapped his arms around Christina in a bear hug. "You're my hero!" he said.

"Sure," said Grant, "she's a real Captain Underpanties."

The sun was setting lazily in the azure sky as the ship returned safely to its dock. Mimi, Papa, and the children thanked Captain Stevens for their safe return, and staggered on sea legs toward their car. Papa carried an ice chest jammed with freshly caught ahi.

Captain Stevens called after them, "Ahoy! You forgot a bag!"

Grant ran back to get it. As he headed back to the car, the bag plopped open. Out rolled a human skull with another message painted on the forehead:

HEED OAHU'S CALL, OR
ALL WILL FALL!

16
CLUES, BLUES

As they made their way back to Hilo, Grant overheard Mimi tell Papa that they needed to go back to Oahu so she could finish her book.

Grant whispered to Christina, "I wish we could just go home. I can't get the picture of that skull out of my mind."

"You heard what Mimi said," Christina said. "She has to write the finale for her book before we go back to the mainland. Besides, I think I know who's behind this whole thing!"

"You do? Who is it?" Grant asked.

"I'm not completely sure," Christina said, "but my suspicions are leading me to Haumea and Kalino's dad."

"Kano?" said Grant. "Don't be silly, Christina. Kano's a very nice man. He wouldn't do anything to hurt his kids' friends. He wasn't even on the same islands when we found most of our clues."

"I don't have all the answers, Grant," Christina admitted, "but we don't really know that much about him, you know."

"You mean you can't come up with anyone else," Grant said.

"Sometimes you're too smart for your own good, little brother!" said Christina.

"I know!" Grant said in a cocky voice. "Of course, I don't have any idea who it could be." He looked **dejected**. He and his sister were usually mystery-solving aces, so what was wrong with their sleuthing powers these days, he wondered.

As Christina lay in bed that night, she tried to figure out the connection between all of the messages, hoping it would lead her to an answer.

Let's see, she thought to herself. There was the creepy man behind the desk at the

Royal Hawaiian that Haumea warned us about, who just *happened* to be named Kamehameha. There was the note, the coconuts, leaves and lizards, scrimshaw, the rock, and now the skull! The only thing that seems to happen is that we keep leaving for another island to get away from each warning. It just doesn't make any sense. She gave up and rolled over to try to get some sleep. Maybe, like Mimi always said, if you put something in your mind and "sleep on it," you often wake up with an answer!

Grant was also trying desperately to come up with some logic for everything that had happened. He thought, the clues all seem to have been written by the same person. Who have we been with the whole..."

"Christina, wake up!" Grant whispered urgently. "I know who's behind everything!"

"Go back to sleep, Grant," said Christina.

"No, I really do!" Grant said, poking Christina's arm.

"Alright, but this better be good," she said, sitting up and rubbing her eyes.

"It's Haumea," Grant said with confidence.

"Haumea? Are you crazy?" Christina said. "Haumea has been a great friend to me. She was with me when you had your surfing accident, so she couldn't have anything to do with this. Have you thought about your friend, Kalino?"

"I think it's you who's crazy!" argued Grant. "Kalino was with me when you had your lava problem so he couldn't have had anything to do with it!"

"I'm sorry, little brother," Christina apologized. "I think we are both exhausted and stressed and need to get a good night's sleep."

"I'm sorry, too," Grant said. "Are we losing our mystery-solving touch so much that we're even accusing our friends?"

"I just hope we can figure this out before it drives us both crazy!" Christina said as she rolled back over. She slept and dreamed of ships and sails, hot lava, poi porridge, and Hawaiian kings.

17
BATTLESHIP BINGO

The next morning was hectic. After a quick breakfast, it was time to head to the airport for their flight back to Oahu. As they started to leave the Pagoda, the skies turned dark and a torrential rain began to fall.

"I've always heard how powerful the rain can be in the Pacific, but I had no idea it could be this intense!" Mimi said.

Strong winds soon followed and swirled violently, scattering bamboo leaves and branches around the property.

"Stay downstairs and away from the windows," Papa shouted, as he closed the door to the guesthouse.

"The rain this time of year usually doesn't last long," Haumea said. "It should be over very soon."

"I hope you're right," said Papa. "There's no way we'll be able to take off in this weather!"

Just as Haumea had predicted, the storm soon ended. Mimi went outside to see if there was any damage to their rented vehicle, while Papa and the kids checked to make sure they had not left anything behind. Mimi came back a moment later, holding what looked like a miniature scale copy of a battleship.

"Is that for me?" Grant said, hoping it was a gift.

"No, Grant, it's not," Mimi replied. "Papa, may I see you on the lanai for a moment?"

Papa followed Mimi as the children watched curiously.

"I found this on the dashboard," Mimi told Papa.

She handed him the toy and pointed to the lettering on the side.

USS *Mystery Girl*, Pearl Harbor, Hawaii, it said. A piece of paper had been taped to the bottom of the ship. It said:

> If you love your life and love your home, return to Oahu and Pearl Harbor to roam. Don't talk to reporters, don't ask questions why, but you'll be too late by the 10th of July!

"What do you think this means, Papa?" Mimi said with concern.

"All I know is that today is July 8th and whatever it is will happen in the next two days," Papa said. "We don't have much time to figure it out. I don't want to scare the kids, but I think we need them to help understand this clue!"

"I agree," Mimi said. "Let's tell them on the way to the airport."

As the *Mystery Girl* made its way toward Oahu, Christina, Grant, Haumea, and Kalino analyzed the toy ship and the note that came with it.

"The letters on this note are the same style as the letters on all of the other clues," Christina observed. "So I still think we're looking for one person behind all of it."

"The ship is a replica of the USS *Arizona*," said Haumea. "I should know. Our dad is superintendent of the memorial!"

"I knew it!" Christina said.

"Knew what?" Haumea asked.

"Uh, I thought it was a replica of the *Arizona*," Christina replied, as Grant raised his eyebrows.

Christina excused herself and went to the cockpit to have a quiet chat with Mimi and Papa.

"I'm still not sure *what's* going to happen on Oahu," Christina began, "but I know *who* we need to watch out for."

"Well, don't keep us in suspense!" Papa said eagerly.

"Kano is behind all of it," Christina said confidently. "He is the superintendent at the

USS *Arizona* memorial. Haumea just confirmed that the toy ship is a replica of the *Arizona* and I told Grant just the other night that I had a bad feeling about him!"

"Kano?" Papa said. "That nice man wouldn't harm anyone. I don't think we should be accusing him of anything without proof."

"Hang on, Papa," Mimi said. "What do we *really* know about him?"

"That's exactly what I was thinking, Mimi!" Christina said. "I mean he is kind of a mystery to us, isn't he?"

"Yes, but I agree with Papa," said Mimi. "He is a very nice man and, as I have always said, we shouldn't accuse anyone unjustly. But let's keep an eye on him anyway! By the way, don't mention anything to Haumea or Kalino."

"I won't even tell Grant," Christina promised. "He's been known to have loose lips. And you know what they always say..."

"LOOSE LIPS SINK SHIPS!" Mimi and Christina cried together.

"What *am* I going to do with you two?" Papa groaned. They had learned the expression from him!

18
OA-WHO?

The *Mystery Girl* landed at Honolulu International at noon, after receiving clearance from the tower. As they exited the plane, Mimi pulled Christina aside and reminded her not to tell Grant, Haumea, or Kalino about their suspicions. Papa called Kano and asked him to pick up Haumea and Kalino at the airport because he and Mimi had planned a "family outing."

Kano arrived at the hangar and greeted everyone.

"How did you enjoy Hilo?" he asked.

"It was great," Christina answered.

"We had a terrible storm," added Kalino.

"I'm glad to be home," Haumea said.

"I wish I was home!" Grant said with sad eyes.

"Well, you have all traveled a long way and even though adventures can be exciting, they are exhausting as well," Kano admitted. "I know how tired we are when we go to the mainland. My wife, Lani, and I would like to invite you all to our home tonight for a traditional Hawaiian dinner. It's our way of saying thank you for showing the kids such a great time."

"That is very kind of you, Kano, but I think we already have plans tonight, don't we, honey?" Papa said to Mimi.

Mimi surprised Papa by saying, "We don't have any plans! We would love to join you for dinner, right, kids?"

"Uh, sure, Mimi," Christina said, puzzled.

Papa said hesitantly, "Well, I'm not so sure..."

"Poi and stuff, Papa!" Grant said. "Let's go!"

"What time should we be there, Kano?" Mimi asked.

"Seven-thirty would be great," Kano replied.

"May we bring anything?" Mimi asked.

"No, thank you," Kano said. "Your presence is all we'll need."

Papa was obviously confused and upset. He was silent during the drive to the new hotel. Grant wondered if he had said something wrong, but didn't want to ask. Only Christina and Mimi were talkative on the ride, discussing which new Hawaiian outfit they would wear that night.

After they checked in, Papa gave Christina and Grant 10 dollars and sent them to have ice cream down at the refreshment stand in the lobby. "Stay there until I come to get you, do you understand?" he said sternly.

"Yes, sir," Christina replied with a sigh.

When they left, Papa turned to Mimi and said, "What were you thinking when you accepted that dinner invitation? By the time we get to dinner we will have less than 24 hours until whatever is going to happen to whomever it's going to happen to! And to go ahead and agree to spend more time with the very man you suspect is behind this whole thing, whatever that is, just seems crazy!"

"Calm down, Papa," begged Mimi. "Let me explain. If Kano actually is the person who's planning whatever is being planned, shouldn't we stay close to him to find out what he's up to?"

Papa groaned. "You're starting to sound like Christina, I mean Grant, I mean I don't know anything anymore. You may be right. He wouldn't want to do anything drastic in front of his family. Now look what you've done! You have me acting like Kano is a bad guy!"

Christina was enjoying her ice cream when Grant gave her a serious look. "What the heck is going on? You and Papa and Mimi have secret meetings on the *Mystery Girl*. Papa is mad and Mimi is acting strange."

"There goes that vivid imagination of yours again, little brother," Christina said. "Just enjoy your ice cream and forget about those crazy ideas."

Grant nodded, but knew there was more that Christina was not telling him.

Papa walked out of the lobby elevator to find Grant and Christina to let them know that it was all right to come back to the room. As he crossed the lobby, Papa noticed that Kano was at the front desk, talking with the desk clerk. Papa picked up his pace to see what was going on, but Kano left the lobby, trotting to a car that was waiting for him. Papa approached the desk clerk and asked him if he knew the man that he had been talking with.

"No, sir," the clerk replied. "He was just asking if we sold coconuts in the gift shop."

Coconuts? Papa was now starting to believe what Christina and Mimi had felt for a while—Kano was up to no good!

Later that evening, the taxi pulled up to Kano and Lani's house, which was on the edge of a canyon overlooking the Pacific Ocean. Mimi rang the doorbell and Haumea opened the door.

"Aloha! Welcome to our home," Haumea said. "Let me tell my parents you're here."

The house was modern, with many statues and Hawaiian artifacts. The view of the ocean was awesome. And the house smelled of cedar, flowers, and something wonderful cooking on the outdoor grill.

"Glad you could make it," Kano said, entering the room. "Let me introduce you to my beautiful wife, Lani."

"It's a pleasure to meet you," Lani said. "I have heard so much about all of you that I feel like I know you already! Please, have a seat."

Kalino ran into the hallway and said, "Come on, guys—let me show you my room!" The kids followed him up an open staircase, and the adults sat down to talk.

"Fresh coconut, anyone?" Lani asked.

"Uh, no, thank you," said Papa. "I'll save my appetite for the main course."

Papa got right down to what he would call 'brass tacks.' "So, Kano, tell me about your job with the USS *Arizona*."

"I work directly for the U.S. National Parks Service, which has operated the memorial and shore-side visitor center since 1980. I am responsible for all functions and staff for both," said Kano.

"I noticed you have your own plane," Mimi said. "Where did you learn to fly?"

"I served in the U.S. Navy as a fighter pilot," Kano said proudly. "I continued to fly after I got out of the service and eventually saved enough money to purchase the *Makani*."

Everyone had a pleasant evening, even those with secret suspicions about their host. After dinner, Kano and Lani presented Mimi and Papa with a gift-wrapped box.

"We sincerely appreciate you both taking such good care of our children and would like you to accept this as a token of our appreciation," Kano said.

As the kids watched eagerly, Mimi unwrapped the box and handed it to Papa to open. Papa fumbled with the lid, then opened the box and pulled out their gift.

"Scrimshaw?" said Papa. "Uh, I mean scrimshaw, how wonderful!"

"Beautiful!" said Mimi, with a funny smile.

"Sure is," added Christina, though she did not sound sincere.

"Just hunky-dory," said Grant. "Just what we wanted."

19

PACIFIC PEARL

On the drive back to the hotel, Christina studied the etching on the scrimshaw that depicted the USS *Arizona*. It was dated July 10. At the bottom of the box was an engraved invitation that read: For Papa.

Papa opened the invitation. "If you want to solve the mystery and save your family, come to the USS *Arizona* tomorrow, at 8 p.m. sharp," he read. "Do not bring your family. You must come alone. We are watching. Tell no one. Or else."

Mimi took the invitation out of Papa's hand to study it. Christina peered over her shoulder.

"The lettering on this invitation is the same as all of the other clues!" Christina said. "You're right, Christina," said Mimi. "I don't think you should go there alone, Papa. It may be dangerous."

"I have to go!" said Papa. "You read the note. There is *nothing* that is too risky when it comes to the safety of my family! Besides, for better or worse, we'll finally find out what all of these clues mean."

"Isn't there some way we can help, Papa?" asked Grant, with concern in his voice.

"No," Papa insisted. "There are times when a man needs to go it alone and this is one of those times."

When they arrived at the hotel, they were surprised to see Haumea and Kalino waiting for them in the lobby.

"What are you two doing here?" Christina asked. "We just left your house."

"Dad had to run a couple of errands in this area, so we came along and thought we'd surprise you!" Kalino said.

"Mimi, if we promise to stay close, can we sit on the beach with Haumea and Kalino?" Christina asked.

"As long as you stay close and that means this beach! Do you understand?" Mimi said.

"Yes, Mimi...close...beach," Christina replied.

Mimi and Papa went to their room and the kids sat down on the sand to talk.

"Haumea, I need to ask you a few questions and I want you to be completely honest with me," Christina said.

"I'm always honest, Christina. What do you want to know?" Haumea asked.

"What does your dad really do for work?" Christina said, looking into Haumea's eyes.

"He's the superintendent at the memorial, just like he said. Why?" asked Haumea, puzzled.

"What does he do in his spare time?" Christina asked.

"He flies his plane, spends time with us, and does scrimshaw etchings," Haumea said.

"Why didn't you tell us that when Grant found the bone that had 'danger' written on it in Maui?" Christina said sternly.

Haumea acted insulted. "You didn't ask and I didn't want to brag. Why are you asking me these questions anyway?"

"There was a note in the gift box your dad gave Papa tonight that makes me think your dad is behind all of the mysterious clues that we've found," Christina said. "Are you sure there's nothing you want to tell me?"

Haumea looked at Kalino and said, "It's time we tell them the truth."

Reluctantly, Kalino nodded in agreement.

Back in the hotel room, Mimi made Papa a fresh cup of herbal tea, trying to help calm his nerves.

"My brave, brave man," Mimi said. "As much as I would like to be with you tomorrow night, I think you are doing the right thing by going alone. That note was very specific and we wouldn't want to put the children in harm's way. I know that you will get through it, but I will pray for your safety anyway," Mimi added.

"I just don't understand what Kano wants from me," Papa said. "Why would you invite the man you are planning to, uh, do whatever to, to eat at your house the night before you do whatever it is you're going to do?"

"They always say to keep your friends close, but your enemies closer," Mimi reminded him. "Maybe it won't be as bad as we're making it out to be," she added hopefully.

"Easy for you to say," Papa said, as he sat down at the computer to study the layout of the memorial.

Even though it had happened many years before, it made Papa sad when he read the website introduction. "On an otherwise calm Sunday morning on December 7, 1941, Japanese warplanes bombed the naval base known as Pearl Harbor."

Papa remembered that eight battleships were sunk and 1,177 crewmembers of the

Navy battleship USS *Arizona* lost their lives that day. He knew that the USS *Arizona* Memorial opened in 1962 and was created to honor and remember all those brave Americans.

As he read, Papa learned that the memorial is 184 feet long. It is divided into three main sections: the entry and assembly rooms; a central area designed for ceremonies and general observation; and the shrine room, where the names of those killed on the *Arizona* are engraved on a marble wall. Papa studied a map of the memorial and committed it to memory.

"I'm as ready as I'll ever be," Papa said, feeling he was preparing for battle.

"I have faith in you," Mimi said, hugging Papa firmly.

Papa, Mimi, and the children slept in the next morning. After a late breakfast, Mimi announced that she would be taking the kids to Diamond Head for an afternoon hike.

"I can't wait to see how big its ears are," Grant joked.

"I can't wait until your jokes get better!" Christina groaned.

"Papa, make sure you take your cell phone and call me to let me know that you're safe," Mimi said. Grant and Christina give Papa a hug and wished him well on his lonely adventure.

"I love you, Papa!" Christina and Grant said at the same time.

"I love you both, too," said Papa. "No matter what happens, don't ever forget that!" he added.

Later that night...

The area around the memorial was well lit, which gave Papa some comfort. He could see the white exterior of the memorial out on the water, its reflection dancing on the waves. As he approached the visitor center, Papa could see that it was mostly dark, with one small light shining at the entrance. Papa pressed against the door and it opened. He saw a message taped to the front desk:

There is a small motorboat with the number 4 on the back of it. Take the boat to the memorial and await instruction.

Papa started the motor and steered the boat toward the memorial. When he arrived at the structure, he saw the shadow of a person who called out, "Come aboard, walk to the central area and carefully open the door."

The memorial was silent and Papa cautiously followed the man's instructions. He stopped in front of the door, took a deep breath, and opened the door.

"SURPRISE!!!!!!" a large group of people yelled. At the very front of the room stood Mimi, Christina, Grant, Kano, Lani, Haumea, and Kalino. As he looked behind them, Papa recognized many of the other men in the room. A banner on the back wall read,

"Happy Anniversary to the Brave Men of Battalion 5."

"Mimi!" Papa shouted with relief. "It was you behind this from the start! You had me half scared to death!"

"I know that you are not big on reunions," Mimi said. "I figured you would not have agreed to come if I'd told you the real reason I wanted to come to Hawaii. So with Kano's help, I set it all up! When the kids started finding the clues, instead of you, well, they finally figured it out, so we were all in on the Big Secret."

Papa spent the rest of the evening catching up with his old military friends and had the time of his life.

Mimi smiled as she watched the man she loved enjoying himself. She thought, "HMMMM. This would make a great mystery book!"

20
SPILLED BEANS

The next morning, Papa awoke feeling rested and at ease for the first time in what seemed like forever.

"Good morning, Papa!" Mimi said cheerfully. Grant and Christina joined them and together gave Papa a huge hug.

"Good morning, you mystery rascals, you!" Papa said.

"Did you enjoy the surprise reunion, Papa?" Grant asked.

"I had the time of my life, once my heart stopped beating like a drum!" Papa said. "You guys could work for the FBI, to have been able to pull this off. You kids didn't know, did you?"

"Not at all, Papa," Christina said. "We had no idea until Haumea and Kalino let us in on it outside the hotel."

"But if you kids hadn't found all the clues and started your grandfather on the mystery trail, I don't know if this would have ever worked out," Mimi insisted.

Grant said, "The clues were so creepy, I was still afraid that you wouldn't make it out of the memorial in one piece!"

"By the way, how was Diamond Head?" Papa asked.

"Diamond Head? We didn't go to Diamond Head, silly," Mimi said. "We had to set up for the party!"

"Wow, I can't believe all of the planning this must have taken," Papa said.

"Being **devious** is an art!" said Mimi, with a wink.

"So is solving mysteries," said Christina.

"Yeah," said Grant. "For a little while, Christina and I were worried we had lost our mystery-solving touch."

"NEVER!" squealed Mimi and Papa together.

"Let's talk about it over breakfast," Mimi said. "We're meeting Kano and his family for brunch at the Hawaiian Village."

"Sounds good to me," Papa said. "I could eat a Hawaiian horse!"

"Who knows?" Grant said. "With all this strange tropical food, you just might!"

The restaurant at the Hawaiian Village was open-air and sat on the edge of Waikiki Beach. Birds outside jostled for crumbs and the scent of coconut tanning lotion wafted through the air. A server, wearing a black muumuu with red and white flowers, led them to a table near the beach. As they were being seated, Kano and his family arrived, carrying four beautiful leis.

As Lani placed them around Papa's, Mimi's, Christina's, and Grant's necks, Kano played a soft tune on his ukulele, while Haumea read a poem:

> *Misty rain sooth the mountains*
> *Golden sunrays warm the sand*

Soft winds cradle the hibiscus blossom
Remember Oahu, our beloved land.

"That was beautiful, Haumea. Where did you learn that?" asked Christina.

"I wrote it myself," Haumea replied. "Seems there's no end to your family's talents," Papa said in admiration.

"Thank you," Haumea said.

The buffet at the restaurant was unlike anything Grant had ever seen. Rows of fresh mango, pineapple, and papaya were followed by a variety of egg dishes, meats, breads, and desserts. There was also a long section of traditional Hawaiian dishes including exotic fish, rice, and, of course, poi!

"I could eat here every day for the rest of my life!" Grant said.

Back at the table, Mimi and Kano proceeded to tell Papa about how the reunion came to be and how they set up the elaborate scheme to keep him guessing.

"You received a letter from your old battalion announcing plans for a reunion," Mimi said. "I opened it by mistake and knew you probably would have thrown it away, just like every other reunion invitation you've ever received. Since it was being held at the USS *Arizona* and we'd been talking about a vacation in Hawaii anyway, I decided to plan it as a surprise. I had met Kano at a book signing in California a few months before and remembered he was in charge of the memorial. So I gave him a call to be my partner in crime."

"I was thrilled to hear from Mimi again," Kano said. "We had talked about my scrimshaw hobby at the book signing. She asked if I would be willing to do all of the etching and lettering for the clues. I couldn't refuse!" he added.

"Well, how did you get..." Papa began. "Ooooh, the big luggage bag! You had me lugging all of the clues around Hawaii, and I didn't even know it! Now that I think about it, that bag did seem to get lighter and lighter as we went along. But I never suspected a thing!"

"Well, this has turned into a great vacation," Christina said. "I got to see Hawaii, met a new best friend, and worked on a pretty scary mystery that turned out to have a very happy ending!"

"It's been a great vacation for me, too!" Grant said. "I also met a great friend, learned to surf, almost crashed in a helicopter, and even went on an ocean adventure! But wait a minute! We never did take our hike on Diamond Neck!"

"For the last time, it's DIAMOND HEAD, DIAMOND HEAD!" Christina said with frustration.

"Whatever!" Grant said with a sly smile.

"It gives you a great excuse to come back to visit," Lani reminded him.

"THAT'S TRUE!" all the kids said together.

"Well," said Papa, "I guess reunions could be arranged every year?"

"Let's bring our cousins Avery, Ella, and Evan next year!" Christina begged.

"Let's come in time for the big surf competition," pleaded Grant.

"I thought we might come back in time for the big Poi Festival," Mimi said with a pout.

"Aloha, ha, ha!" said Grant.

Well, that was fun!

Wow, glad we solved that mystery!

Where shall we go next?

EVERYWHERE!

The End

Aloha, Hawaii
by Christina

One thing about travel is what you think about a place is often very different from what it is really like. Hawaii is beautiful, there's no doubt about that. And the people are so friendly. I do not know if I would like living in such a lovely, but isolated place. However, it was interesting to learn that many Hawaiians would like to have their own nation because they feel that they were made a state against their will. Having been there now, I can understand that there are always two sides to every opinion. I will watch the news and see how this part of Hawaii's amazing history works out. I am sure that Mimi and Papa will insist I do! Aloha!

Now...go to

www.carolemarshmysteries.com
and...

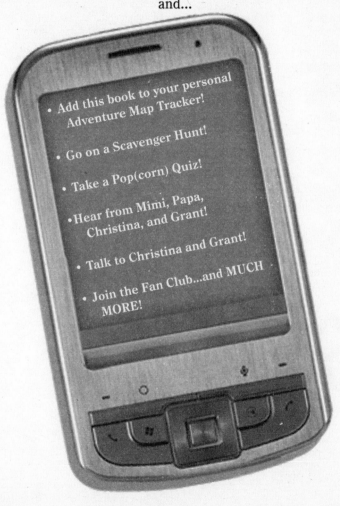

- Add this book to your personal Adventure Map Tracker!

- Go on a Scavenger Hunt!

- Take a Pop(corn) Quiz!

- Hear from Mimi, Papa, Christina, and Grant!

- Talk to Christina and Grant!

- Join the Fan Club...and MUCH MORE!

GLOSSARY

aloha: a Hawaiian greeting or farewell, meaning "love"

hula: a traditional Hawaiian dance that tells a story

lava: liquid rock pouring from an active volcano

lei: a necklace of flowers used to greet people in Hawaii

leprosy: a skin disease causing loss of feeling and tissue; now known as Hansen's disease

luau: a beachside feast with dancing and a smoked pig

poi: a food made by pounding taro roots into a paste

surfing: riding on top of waves balanced on a long board

telescope: an instrument used to view objects in space

SAT GLOSSARY

flora: flowers

ornate: very detailed, or complex

altitude: how far above sea level a place is

deject: to put aside

devious: dishonest, or underhanded

Enjoy this exciting excerpt from:

THE MYSTERY

ON THE

Great

Lakes

1
WHEN BUFFALOES FLY

Christina wiped her mouth with a bright yellow napkin. The spicy hot sauce from the Buffalo wings stung her lips and tickled her tongue. Her blue eyes watered until tears streaked her cheeks.

Grant grinned, his mouth coated with greasy orange sauce. "These are great! But I didn't know buffaloes had wings." Buffalo sauce covered his hands and trickled down his arms to his elbows.

"Eww, Grant," Christina said. She handed him a napkin.

Mimi laughed. "Glad you like them," she said, "but buffaloes don't have wings. Buffalo wings are chicken. They're named

Buffalo wings because they were created right here, in Buffalo, New York!"

Even eating the messy Buffalo wings, Mimi kept her white ruffled blouse and red suit jacket spotless. She somehow didn't seem bothered by the super-spicy hot sauce either.

Papa took several long gulps of lemonade. He'd ordered the hottest hot wings, and from the look on his face, they were fiery hot! Of course, Mimi always said he had a mouth made of stainless steel. He could eat—and enjoy—even hot jalapeño peppers.

"Papa, when are we going to see the Rock and Roll Hall of Fame?" Christina asked.

"We'll be there in no time," Papa replied, his voice hoarse from the hot sauce. "We're just about ready to kick off our tour of the Great Lakes!"

Grant and Christina often traveled with their mystery-writing grandmother, Mimi, as she did research for her books. Her latest book was to be set on the Great Lakes. Their grandfather, Papa, flew the family wherever they needed to go in his red-and-white airplane, the *Mystery Girl*. Mimi affectionately referred to him as the "cowboy pilot" in his Stetson hat, jeans, and leather boots.

Papa took one last gulp from his tall drink. "Once we finish lunch," he explained, "we're off to board the *Mystery Girl*. She'll take us over to Cleveland and Lake Erie."

"*Eeeeerie*?? That's a creepy name for a lake. Where were we earlier today?" Grant asked.

"Lake Ontario," Christina said. Don't you remember, Papa said our route would be Lake Ontario, then southwest to Lake Erie, then north to Lake Huron, then more north to Lake Superior, then south to Lake Michigan, or vice versa, I forget."

Grant groaned. "Well, I'm lost already. I can see I won't be able to write my 'What I Did on My Vacation' report next year in school without a big, giant map!"

"Niagara Falls sure was pretty this morning," Papa said. He wiped a bead of sweat from his brow, still feeling the effects of the hot sauce. He grabbed his cowboy hat and fanned his face.

Mimi nodded, a tiny smear of sauce on her chin.

"I liked seeing the rainbow over the falls and getting wet from the mist. That was awesome!" Grant said.

"So, Mimi," Grant continued, "what makes the Great Lakes so great?"

"Well, where do I start?" Mimi said. "One of the main things you should know is that the Great Lakes hold about 20 percent of the fresh surface water in the world!"

"What's fresh water?" Grant asked. "It must not be the water at my school's water fountain, because it tastes old!"

Mimi laughed. "No, Grant," she said. "Fresh water is water on the earth that is not sea water from the ocean. It's found in lakes, rivers, streams...places like that. It's very important for the survival of people and animals on the earth."

DING! A text message arrived on Mimi's cell phone. "I wonder who that could be?" she said, and peered at her bright red phone.

"Oh, it's Ichabod, the lighthouse keeper!" Mimi read the message. She frowned. "Hmm, he seems a bit worried about the lighthouse. Something about odd noises in the night. Not like him. I hope he's okay. He's getting older. I'm not sure how much longer he can traipse up and down those lighthouse steps."

Christina and Grant stopped eating. They focused on Mimi.

Mimi snapped her phone shut. "Well, we're set to go see him. He can't wait!" she said with a smile.

Grant elbowed Christina. She leaned in and he whispered, "*Ichabod*. That's a creepy name. Sort of like that Headless Horseman dude?"

"Sure is creepy," Christina agreed.

Grant shook his head bouncing his blonde curls all around. "Sounds almost ...*icky*," he said, scrunching his face.

Christina nodded. "And what about him hearing odd noises? I'm not sure I want to meet Mr. Ichabod after all. Or visit his haunted lighthouse."

Christina hadn't really wanted to go on this trip to the Great Lakes with Mimi and Papa. Even though the fall leaves were spectacular hues of red, yellow, and orange, Christina wished they'd come in the summer so she could swim. Not in the fall, when it was too cold to go in the water, at least not on purpose! Now with the idea of spending time with a creepy lighthouse keeper, Christina wanted nothing more to do with the Great Lakes, and they'd hardly begun their journey.

Papa paid the bill and they left the restaurant. Soon, they were aboard the *Mystery Girl*.

"Where are we going now?" Grant asked.

"To Cleveland, Ohio, and Lake Erie," Papa replied.

"And the Rock and Roll Hall of Fame!" Christina added. She was a true rock and roll music lover. She couldn't wait to see all the guitars on display.

"So, we're not going to see Mr. Icky?" Grant asked.

Papa laughed. "Do you mean Mr. Ichabod?"

"Oops, yeah, Mr. Ichabod. Sorry, Papa," Grant said.

"We'll see him later in the trip, Grant," Mimi said.

"Let's get this plane up in the air! Let's rock and roll!" Papa cried, and the *Mystery Girl* launched into the crisp, bright blue autumn sky.

Grant played air guitar in his seat, bounding from side to side. At the end of his animated guitar solo, Grant shouted in his best Elvis Presley impersonation, "Thank you! Thank you very much!"

He bowed to the pretend crowd that had come to hear him play, flinging his arms to the side. WHACK! He accidentally hit Christina's shoulder.

"Ouch! Quit it, Grant!" Christina cried.

DING! DING! A text message suddenly appeared on Christina's cell phone. *Who could that be from*, she thought. Her eyes grew wide when she opened her phone to read it.

The text message said,

> BEWARE OF BESSIE, THE
> EERIE MONSTER!

Christina immediately nudged Grant. "Look at this!" she whispered.

"Who is that from?" Grant asked.

Christina looked a second time at the message. There was no signature.

"I don't know," she replied and shrugged. "It doesn't say. Let me see what phone number sent it." Christina checked the number. Her mouth dropped open. "There isn't one!"

Goose bumps rose on Grant's arm. His big blue eyes grew wide with concern. "Maybe it's the Erie monster?"

Christina felt a chill, and pulled her sweater around her. "I sure hope not, because that's exactly where we're headed!"